Christopher P.N. Maselli

09 08 07 06 05 04 03 02 01   10 9 8 7 6 5 4 3 2 1

Wichita Slim's Campfire Stories
ISBN 1-57562-542-3   Product #30-1213 ©2001

©2001 Kenneth Copeland Publications

Published by Kenneth Copeland Publications
Fort Worth, TX 76192-0001

Larry Warren/cover art

Stories

The Good News

1

**Wichita was very excited to hear what
his friend, Bob Statler, had to say.**

"Wichita Slim! Wichita Slim! Wichita Slim!"

The marshal didn't look up at the approaching horse and rider immediately...but he should have. Before he knew it, he was lifted high off the sandy ground in an unexpected embrace. It was his good friend, Bob Statler. Big, round, and almost always in good spirits, Statler was a little happier than usual this sunny afternoon.

"Put me down, Bob!" Wichita said after a courteous laugh. "What in blazes are you so excited about?"

"Marshal, you'll never guess what happened to me!" he said without losing a moment's excitement.

"No, I don't reckon I will," Wichita acknowledged. "But I bet you're about to tell me." Wichita knew Bob hadn't come clear to the outskirts of town to find him and keep a secret.

"I was just healed, Marshal!" Bob said enthusiastically. "God healed my back! See?"

The cowboy bent over several times in a row, touching his fingertips to his toes—with no back pain whatsoever.

"Your *back*—didn't you tell me one of the horses you were training bucked you off a few years ago?" Wichita wondered aloud. Wichita knew that Bob used to train horses, until one day a horse threw him off his back. Bob hit the ground with such an impact that his back had hurt him ever since...especially when he bent over.

"That's right!" Bob said without losing a breath, "I hit my back on the ground as hard as a hoof hits dirt! Well, I prayed today—believed God—and He healed me!"

"Well, praise God!" Wichita exclaimed and then chuckled. "Aren't you glad He's in the business of healing?" Bob nodded and touched his toes again. It felt so good to touch his toes without pain—Bob was truly thankful at what God had done. "Well, I suppose you've been telling everyone," Wichita added.

"Well, uh, no," Statler stopped stretching. He had hoped Wichita wouldn't mention telling others. "I thought it'd be all right to tell you...but what would others think? Especially if they weren't Christians?" Statler asked.

Wichita couldn't believe what he was hearing—that Statler actually thought he shouldn't tell anyone he was healed!

"What would others think?!" Wichita challenged. "Statler, they need to know! They're hurting inside and outside. They need people like you and me, who know God heals, to tell them. If we don't, maybe *no one* will!"

Statler was a little shocked at Wichita's reaction. But he knew the marshal was right—even if others might not believe him. Jesus didn't want people sick and hurting—the devil did. And Bob realized it was his responsibility to tell them that Jesus is Lord over sickness...and God has the desire and power to heal them.

"Bob," the marshal encouraged, "you just need to do what you believe the Spirit of God is saying to you in your heart." Bob thought about that long and hard. *What is God telling me in my heart?* he wondered. Then he felt a boldness—strong and deep inside him—that caused him to stand up straight and tall.

"You're right, Marshal! I'm going to tell everyone I meet about my healed back! It's not right that I go on like nothing happened when something *did* happen...something that changed my life!"

Wichita Slim placed a firm grasp on Statler's shoulder.

"Good for you, Statler," Wichita commended. "And if *one* life is touched because of that miracle, then it's worth telling a million more."

Bob nodded in agreement. Then, in one swift motion, Wichita Slim hopped on his stallion's saddle and turned around to leave.

"Where you going?" asked Statler, a little surprised at Wichita's sudden escape.

"Well, I thought we had some good news to spread!" Wichita answered. Statler smiled and tipped his hat towards Slim, still feeling the strength inside.

"Marshal, you got that right!" Statler mounted his own horse.

Almost in unison, the men shouted a confident "Yah!" and their horses shot forward into town.

2

**Shane learned that playing near danger
may not be as fun as it looks.**

"Let's do it!" said Shane Decker excitedly.

"Shane!" his sister, Shauna, protested. "You know we're not supposed to play this close to the end of the ridge—Marshal said!" But Shane just laughed.

"His name's 'Wichita,' not 'Marshal,'" Shane corrected. "Besides, I'm not gonna fall. I've seen Luis do it before."

"Yea," Shauna admitted, "but Luis is 16—you're 11. And Marshal said we weren't supposed to come this close to the ridge!" Shane always liked to be a little daring, but Shauna knew that sometimes his curiosity got him into bad situations. And Shady Canyon wasn't a place to play around...at least that's what Wichita Slim had said.

Shane squinted his eyes as the sun beat down upon his face.

"Come on, Shauna, it's fun!" Shane said, assuringly. "I'll do your chores if you come."

Seven-year-old Shauna stood tall and placed her hands on her hips. "Risk my life and you'll do my chores? I don't think so." Her brother rolled his eyes.

"Whatever," he said, continuing to play. Shauna felt sad that her brother didn't want to play with her now, but she didn't want to risk her life...and she didn't want him to risk his life either.

"Come on, Shane, stop playing."

Shane couldn't believe what he was hearing. Here they had a chance to play near the edge of the ridge without anyone getting upset, and Shauna didn't want to! He was determined to show her how fun it was.

Carefully (yet daring), Shane grabbed onto a large rock with one hand and leaned over the edge of the ridge for a look. It was beautiful.

"Shane! Stop it!" Shauna warned. "You could fall!"

"I won't fall..." Shane reassured her. "You should see how beautiful it is."

CHUNK! Suddenly the rock moved—and Shane slid. His heart skipped a beat as he grabbed for the ground.

"Shane!" Shauna jumped up and grabbed his arm and pulled him from the edge. He was silent.

BOOM-BOOM-BOOM-BOOM! A horse and rider came rushing toward them. Wichita Slim jumped off his steed.

"Are you all right?" he asked, concerned.

"Yea," Shane whispered.

"He almost fell off the cliff, Marshal!" Shauna added.

"So I saw," Wichita conceded. "Now you two need to tell me what you're doing here in the first place. Haven't I told you never to play near this canyon?"

Both children were silent.

"God's Word says that when you obey, you'll be given a long life," Wichita said.

"Yeah, well, mine just about ended!" Shane said, still shaken up.

"Well, rules don't exist just to make your life hard, Shane," Wichita continued. "They're here to help you."

"I guess sometimes I need to remember *that* when the rule seems like a punishment," Shane added.

Wichita Slim, Shane and Shauna all stood and walked away from the ridge. Shane felt bad that he had disobeyed—it just seemed like so much fun at the time. He hoped Wichita wasn't mad.

"You won't have to be concerned about us getting near there again," Shane said.

"Yeah," agreed Shauna. Of course, she didn't want to go near that old ridge in the first place.

"Good," said Wichita. "How 'bout we go into town and call it a night?"

"Sounds good, Marshal," Shauna said.

"After that surprise," Shane added, "I'm willing to call it a *year!*"

With a chuckle, Wichita helped his two friends onto his horse and safely walked them away from Shady Canyon.

3

Deputy Rigler felt something was wrong
with his new friendship.

"Oh dear, oh dear!" Deputy Joel Rigler shook his head
as he entered the Eagle Grove U.S. Marshal's Office and
approached Wichita Slim. Wichita was sitting at his desk,
across from a lone, empty jail cell. The sun outside was
setting and Slim had just turned on a kerosene lamp, filling
the room with a strong gassy odor.

"You sound a bit under the weather, Rigler," Wichita said.

"I am," the deputy admitted. "I thought I made a new
friend this last week, but now I just don't know." He pulled
at his long, red mustache.

"Well, you're a pretty good judge of character," Wichita
said. He held out his hand, offering his deputy the seat

across from him. Rigler sat down and pulled his flimsy tie straight.

"I guess so."

"What makes you think you don't have a new friend?" Slim politely asked.

Rigler thought about the question for a moment. "Well, he just likes to fish for trout and tell stories," he finally said.

"Fishing and stories?" the marshal exclaimed, removing his hat and scratching his head. "That sounds all right to me."

"Well, the fishing's fun," Rigler said, "but the stories he tells aren't true—he lies, Slim. And he talks about other people behind their back and cusses...you see, he's not a Christian."

Wichita Slim nodded. "Sounds like you have a problem with light and darkness."

Rigler looked at him and wondered what he meant. When he finally asked, Wichita told him to close the wooden shudders on the windows.

"The Bible says light and darkness don't have a lot in common," Wichita explained. "Let me show you." Then he turned off the kerosene lamp. A hiss and pop sounded and the room filled with darkness.*

Rigler snickered, sounding uneasy. He couldn't see the marshal—in fact, with the midnight black surrounding him, he couldn't see anything.

"Marshal...?" he called out—but there was no response. He reached forward blindly, trying to feel for the knob to ignite the lamp. But before he could find it, a hiss sounded and a blast of light from the lamp made Rigler throw his head sideways and close his eyes as tight as he could.

"Hey!" he shouted. Wichita Slim was chuckling in his chair.

"What?!" Wichita exclaimed, smiling. "Looks like you agree that light and darkness don't mix very well!"

"Yeah..." Rigler said, rubbing his eyes. The Marshal leaned across his desk and whispered to the deputy, "You know, the Bible says in Ephesians 5:8 that we are light in Christ."

Rigler pulled at his mustache as he thought. Suddenly he had a surge of understanding flood his face as he smiled and shook his head at Slim.

"I guess since I'm a Christian and my new friend isn't...well, we're like light and darkness—we don't mix very well."

Wichita leaned back and smiled.

"And," Rigler added, "other than fishing for trout, we probably don't have a lot in common...just like light and darkness."

"The closer we get to God, the less we have in common with the world...it's true," Wichita explained. "But Jesus told us to go into the world and tell them about how they can be saved. And Rigler," he continued, "through your example, you can be a light to your new friend."*

"So I *did* make a new friend?" Deputy Joel Rigler asked.

"I'd be more inclined to say *he* did," Wichita answered matter-of-factly, as he tapped on the lamp.

The deputy smiled. "Well, then, I'm goin' fishin'!"

"For trout?" Wichita wondered as he placed his hat back on his head.

"Nope," Rigler answered as he rose from his chair. "I don't mean *that* kind of fishing—I'm going fishing for a soul!" As abruptly as he had arrived, he left, leaving Wichita shaking his head and smiling.

*2 Corinthians 6:14; Mark 16:15

The Scoop on St. Nick

4

Clara understood the meaning of Christmas when she heard the true story of "Santa Claus."

As soon as Clara Rigler walked into the kitchen, her mouth began to water. Wintertime was the *only* time it snowed in Eagle Grove, Kansas. And snow meant ice cream—and Clara loved it! She was in her bedroom when she heard the *clack, clack* of a metal spoon mixing snow with sugar in a large wooden bowl. Her mother turned around when she heard her 10-year-old daughter approach.

"Want some?" the 32-year-old woman asked, sitting down at the kitchen table and grabbing another spoon. Clara's eyes lit up.

"I want a *big* scoop!" she said with a tint of laughter in her voice. Clara's mother invited her to share the same bowl. Clara immediately dove in and ate three big spoonfuls of ice cream, causing the roof of her mouth to chill. Her mother giggled.

She was so thankful for her daughter. Only a few months ago, Clara was kicked by an alarmed horse and almost died. But God totally healed her when her father, Deputy Joel Rigler, prayed. Clara was indeed a gift from God.

"Tell me a Christmas story, Mama," Clara said. Mrs. Rigler thought for a moment.

"Well, since you're such a special gift from God, let me tell you about someone else whose birth was a great gift to his parents."

Clara listened closely and shoved another melting spoonful of ice cream into her mouth. She loved her mother's stories.

"I'm going to tell you the true story of St. Nicholas—a man who grew up knowing God," Mrs. Rigler said. She put down her spoon.

"Nicholas' parents were Christians and prayed to God for a child," she began. "And just a little later, little Nick was born. His parents considered him to be a gift from God, too.

"They taught him to live for God and to give gifts to the poor. When Nick was in his teens, his parents died—but he never stopped living for Jesus. He even became a priest in the church when he was only 19 years old."

Clara smiled, still filling her mouth with small bites of ice cream. "That's young!" she exclaimed.

"It's not much older than you," her mother said. Then she continued the story. "Soon he became a bishop—a leader in the church. His uncle even prophesied over him and said Nick would help many people and be very blessed. It's even said that St. Nicholas would spend all night studying God's Word so he could bring it to the people."

"Wow!" Clara said between bites of the cold dessert.

"Yeah," Mrs. Rigler agreed, pulling a shawl around her shoulders. "He was known for helping the poor, for praying and for being strong in his faith.

"One time he was caught giving money to a family. But St. Nicholas made the man who caught him promise never to tell anyone. He wanted everyone to give thanks to God for the gifts."

"Hmm. I've never heard all that before," Clara said. She scooped the remaining sugar-water out of the bowl and swallowed it.

"It's true. St. Nicholas is a picture of what Christmas is all about. His life is an example of living for God and giving—because Christmas is about Jesus. He's the *greatest* gift, given to us by God, the real Gift-Giver."

"So why do we call it 'Christmas?'" Clara asked. Her mother paused, closed her eyes and smiled.

"'Christ mass' means 'anointing celebration.' Christmas is a celebration of how God anointed Jesus with the Holy Ghost and power. He came to earth to do good, heal the hurting and give His life for us." She opened her teary eyes and winked at Clara.

"You all right, Mama?" Clara asked.

"I'm just glad God's given us a Merry Christmas, sweetie," her mother replied.

"One more question," Clara said after licking her spoon. "St. Nicholas showed us all about Jesus and giving, right?"

Mrs. Rigler agreed, "That's right."

"Well, how would you like to give me another scoop of

ice cream?" Clara asked. "I'll listen to another story."

Mrs. Rigler looked at her daughter, picked up the bowl and then kissed her on the forehead. As she began to wash the dish, she simply turned to Clara, smiled and said, "Ho! Ho! Ho!"

5

**Shane knew monsters didn't exist...
but then why was he staring one in the face?**

I *know* I heard a bump. I always hear bumps. Bumps and knocks and clicks and clacks—and I always hear them at night, when everyone's asleep. My little redheaded sister, Shauna, sleeps across the room, but the bumps never wake her up...so she's never scared at night. If I wake her up, she just says, "Shane, go to sleep. You didn't hear anything. It's your imagination."

Shauna and I are orphans and don't know where our parents are. Wichita Slim found us abandoned in the desert six years ago when I was only 5 years old. He brought us to Miss Joy Soh because she's a nurse. Well, to make a long story short, we live with her now—and she loves us like she's our real mom. She's not married, but Shauna and I are good company for her and she helps us learn. It's a pretty good arrangement.

But she doesn't hear the bumps either. And neither of them saw the monster. That was the worst. Right after I heard the bump, my eyes shot open and I saw—standing where my bedpost used to be—a large, thin monster wearing a cap. I know it sounds stupid, but that's what I saw. And who says monsters can't wear caps?

Oh, sure. I know there's no such thing as monsters. I'm not *that* young. But whether I believe monsters exist or not, I know I saw one standing in the shadows at the foot of my bed, wearing a cap. I yanked my feet up behind me. I wasn't about to let him eat them. They're *my* feet!

"Shauna!" I let out in a harsh whisper. "Shauna!" One of her eyes opened and the moon reflected off it.

"Shauna!" I whispered again, keeping an eye on the cap-wearing fiend. "There's a monster in the room!"

"Hmmm...imagination..." she mumbled and turned away from me, pulling her covers tightly around her. *Great, I thought, I'm about to get eaten alive and my sister's more interested in her beauty sleep.*

I was just about to call for Miss Soh when the cap moved. My mouth went dry. I knew I shouldn't have left the window open. The wind is irritating him. I knew there was only one thing left to do.

"Mr. Monster?" I whispered, "Let's talk."

He didn't move...so I continued.

"You don't want to eat me," I reasoned with him. "I'm small—only 11 years old. You'll be hungry again in no time." He still didn't move. Was he listening? I knew my argument was ridiculous. After all, this monster was *thin*—and I would be a better dinner for him than nothing at all. I began to shiver.

Suddenly, a gust of wind blew through the window and made the monster even madder. He threw off his cap and revealed a little knobby head. I instantly knew that his brain was so small he didn't understand a thing I was saying. He didn't care. I was a goner. There was nothing left to do but say my prayers.

That's when I felt a surge of boldness rise up inside me.

I had forgotten—I didn't have to be scared. I'm a child of God! And I was protected in God's armor!

"Monster!" I said out loud, sitting up and pointing straight at him. "Get out of our room and never come back! God's Word says I don't have to fear when I lie down to sleep—because God's given me a spirit of power and love and self-control. So you have to leave—in Jesus' Name!"*

As quickly as he arrived, the monster faded into nothing, leaving only my bedpost behind. I breathed deeply and relaxed for a moment and then got up to close the window. *Wow,* I thought, *one Word from God and all monsters have to obey.*

As I shut the window, Shauna turned over and looked at me.

"What are you doing, Shane?" she asked. "Did you say something?"

I paused, picked my cap up off the floor and put it back on the bedpost. Slowly, I felt the wooden grooves on the bedpost and realized there had been no monster there all along—I had just been letting the devil scare me.

"Shane," my sister persisted. "Did something scare you?"

"Go back to sleep—it's your imagination," I replied, and I got back into bed and closed my eyes. For there was nothing to fear.

*Proverbs 3:24; 2 Timothy 1:7

The Rest of the Story

6

**Bob suddenly realized there was more
to Jesus' sacrifice than what he knew.**

"Aww-haww-haww, Wichita!" cried Billy Bob Statler, wiping his dark blue eyes with his fists. Marshal Wichita Slim was walking across the dusty main street of Eagle Grove when Bob caught his attention—and his arm.

"Statler," Wichita said, moving the horse trainer to the side of the road. "What in creation are you cryin' about?"

Statler squeezed his eyes together, forcing out one last sigh and set his eyes on Wichita's. Slim looked back at Bob, slightly squinting from the brightness of the sun. After a short pause Statler spoke.

"Marshal, I finally understand what Jesus did for us."

"Wonderful!" Slim said enthusiastically, lightly

punching Bob in the arm. Bob's mouth dropped open.

"Wonderful?!" he exclaimed. "But it's so sad!" He began to sob again, causing his whole body to shake. Billy Bob was a large, round man and whenever he got excited or cried, his whole body showed it.

"Now wait just a cotton-picking minute, here," Slim interrupted. "What Jesus did for us was miraculous—but maybe you aren't seeing the full picture." Bob didn't seem to hear him.

"Oh, Marshal. Let me tell you," he said. "Jesus did nothing wrong—*nothing*.... In fact, He only helped people."

"Yeah..." Wichita coaxed.

"Then one of His close friends sold out on Him. And everyone thought He was a bad man. They whipped Him and—" Statler took a deep breath and ran his left hand through his wiry, brown hair. He was still looking straight at Wichita as he told his story.

"They made fun of Him and called Him names," he continued. "And then...then do you know what they did?"

"They killed Him," Wichita stated flatly.

"They nailed His hands and feet on a wooden cross and—oh! I can't tell anymore—it's unbearable!"

The Marshal removed his dark hat and bowed his head shortly.

"He sure does love us," he said.

"Yeah," Bob added. "That's just it—He went through all that so that we wouldn't have to die for our sins—all the bad things we've done. He did it for us." Bob wiped his tear-stained eyes and shook his head.

"Well..." Wichita prompted.

"That's it," Statler confirmed. Slim put his hat back on his head.

"You didn't hear what I said, did you?" Slim asked. Billy Bob thought hard for a moment.

"Uh, you said that Jesus really loved us in order to do that."

"What I said," Marshal Wichita Slim explained, "was that He really *does* love us—not *did* love us." Resisting the urge to scratch his head, Statler admitted that he didn't understand.

"Statler! No wonder you're cryin' so! Now Jesus' death is nothing to take lightly—anybody knows that—but you forgot the rest of the story."

"I did?" Statler stood still with a surprised look on his face.

"Sure did," Slim said. "See, Jesus' dying on the cross is only the first half of the story." Bob was all ears.

"Jesus died so we wouldn't have to," Slim continued. "But then three days later He rose again! *Jesus is alive, Bob!*" Bob's eyes became as big as horses' hooves.

"Jesus died so we wouldn't have to—and then He rose again?" Bob asked.

"Yes!" Slim was getting excited now. "Not only that, but when Jesus died, He bore all our sin *and* sickness *and* failure *and* death on the cross with Him. Then He rose from the dead, making death so it would have no effect on us!"

"Wow!" Billy Bob jumped up and down. "I remember when He healed my back last year," he said. "But He really took my sickness a long time ago on the Cross, huh?"

"That's right," Slim said, satisfied that Bob finally understood the rest of the story. Billy Bob could hardly contain his excitement.

"Well, I gotta go tell someone about this," he exclaimed, happily hopping into the middle of the road.

"Jesus is alive!" he said.

Wichita laughed heartily and continued on his journey, knowing ol' Billy Bob Statler would never be the same again.

A BENEFICIAL VISIT

7

**"One-Eyed" Tom Carson was about to find out
no one could take Wichita Slim's most valuable possession.**

Suddenly Slim awoke, staring straight into the crazed, right eye of "One-Eyed" Tom Carson. The black patch over Carson's other eye blended into the darkness of the room. Slim could feel the all-too-familiar, icy-metal circle of Carson's pistol pressed into his neck.

"Early mornin' to you, Slim," Carson whispered. "Sorry to bother you while you're all tucked in." Slim stayed quiet and glanced over at his own gun, lying underneath the newly lit lamp beside his bed.

"Oh, I wouldn't reach for that if I were you," Carson said louder this time. "Sometimes I can be a little 'trigger-happy,' especially when there's a full moon."

Slim peered at him. "You wouldn't hurt a fly."

"True. But then again, a fly hasn't sent me to jail as many times as you have, Marshal!"

"Speaking of jail, isn't that where you're supposed to be right now?"

"Oh, you know," Carson said casually. "Some law-*maker* puts me in. Some law-*breaker* gets me out."

Slim let out a long breath, confident Carson wouldn't fire his weapon. "One-Eyed" Tom Carson was only a troublemaker, a menace and a robber—never a killer. But it was better to play it safe.

"So to what do I owe this pleasure?" Slim inquired.

"Well, as I left jail, I thought to myself, *Who should I visit?* Then I thought of you—because you've *helped me* so much in the past," Carson mocked.

"What do you want, Tom?"

"Hmm..." Carson said, getting up and wandering around the one-room house, careful to keep his gun pointed at Slim. "Let's shoot for the stars. Give me what's most valuable to you."

For the first time, Slim laughed. "You can't take it. No one can take *that* away from me."

Carson scowled. Slim sat up in his bed, moving closer to his weapon.

"Don't even *think* about it," Carson warned. "Now what is it that's so valuable?"

"My salvation," Wichita stated.

Tom let out a whooping howl. *"What?* What good is your salvation here on earth?"

"Well, it's better than any *thing*, that's for sure."

"Yea, right."

"Carson, let me tell you about God's benefits of salvation.

While you're out stealing and waking people up in the middle of the night, I'm sleeping in peace. That's one benefit right there."

"That's it?" Carson asked.

"No," Wichita said. "God forgives me of all my sins. He heals my diseases and protects me. He loads me with love and mercy. He gives me good things." Carson stayed quiet, not sure how to respond.*

"One more thing," Wichita said. "He makes me strong and overcoming—like an eagle."

In one, swift move, Marshal Wichita Slim grabbed his gun and pointed it straight at "One-Eyed" Tom Carson. "Care for a draw?" Wichita asked.

Carson thought for a moment, keeping his pistol aimed at Slim. "Well, it seems you have nothing I'm interested in," he said. "I'd better be going."

"Tom, you walk out that door and I'll have to fire—it's my duty."

Carson winked and opened the door. Wichita aimed his gun at Carson's arm and fired.

Nothing happened.

Carson opened his left hand, revealing six bullets. "What? You don't think I took the necessary precautions, Marshal? I took the bullets out of your gun before I woke you."

Quickly, Carson escaped out the door of Slim's house. By the time Slim reached the opening, the street was quiet and dark.

"Well, Carson, you may have got away," Slim whispered to himself. "But whether you realize it or not, God knows where you are. And you just left here with more than my bullets. You know a little bit more about the God Who loves you—and that Word will stay with you forever."

Yawning, Slim closed his door, shook his head and went back to bed. For him, it had been a good night.

*Psalm 103

HIDDEN IN THE GROVE

8

**Wichita Slim wasn't sure who—or what—
he'd find in the forest outside town.**

Wichita Slim crept through the woods on the edge of Eagle Grove. Carefully, he pushed aside long branches of oak trees that stood confident in the sunlight. Earlier that morning, Billy Bob Statler was sure he heard snoring coming from these woods. And everyone knew what that meant...outlaws were making camp under the cover of the forest. That's why Wichita proceeded with caution. You never know whose face (or gun barrel) might be on the other side of the nearest—

Crunch...

Wichita held his breath and then let it out slowly.

Crunch...Crunch...BLAM!

Slim hit the dirt as a tree branch beside him was sliced in half. He quickly lifted up his rifle as he landed on his belly. He peered through the sight, looking for the cause of the shot he heard. But there was nothing.

"Hello, Slim."

Slim flipped over onto his back, aiming his rifle at the voice.

"'One-Eyed' Tom Carson," he said as he rose, keeping his rifle steadily on his target.

"So we meet again," Carson acknowledged.

"Put down your weapon," the marshal said with authority. "Or, if you care to get in a gunfight, we can see who's the better shot."

"Hmmmf," Tom Carson huffed as he thought for a moment. Then he dropped his weapon onto the ground. "Everyone knows you're the best shot in these parts."

"Good choice," Wichita said. "Now *what* in the world are you doing out here? You escaped last night and could have run *anywhere!* But instead you stay near town?"

'One-Eyed' Tom Carson brushed his forehead with his wrist and adjusted his eye patch. "Where would I go?" he said bitterly. "I don't have any cash. Your house didn't have anything worth taking, remember? Or did you forget about my little visit while you were in bed—without your gun—so early in the morning?"

"Well, things have changed now, haven't they? Now *my* gun is pointed toward *you* instead of *yours* being pointed toward *me.*"

"Things sure *have* changed," Carson said, looking up at the cloudless, blue sky. "Bet you won't be religious anymore—now that *you're* the one with the gun."

"Carson, you'll never learn, will you. When I witnessed to you last night about God's salvation, it was because I knew you needed Him—everyone does."*

"Yea, but *He* doesn't need *me.*"

"He loves you—in fact, God sent His only Son to die for you."*

"What for?" Tom asked with a scoff.

"Jesus came and died for you so that you wouldn't have to die for all the robbing, cheating and lying you've done, Carson. If you want to know Him, all you have to do is pray. Say, 'God, I'm sorry for all the bad I've done—I want to change. I want You to be the Lord of my life today.'"*

Wichita kept his gun steady. Carson stood silent for a long moment.

"So are you going to throw me in jail?" he wondered.

"That's my duty," Slim affirmed.

The robber shifted his feet and looked down at the ground. Then, putting his hands behind his back, he said, "Then take me in and get it over with, Marshal. I don't want your God." Slim lowered his rifle and reached for a small rope, tied to his belt.

Suddenly, 'One-Eyed' pulled his hands out from behind his back, pointing a miniature gun at Slim. "Well, well, Marshal. It looks like I'm prepared...*again*—and you're caught helpless...*again.*" It was true. Slim lowered his head and dropped his rifle.

"You got me, Tom," he said.

Tom laughed triumphantly. "I got Wichita Slim! I actually have the legend! And this time, I'm not going to let you get away!" He pointed his miniature gun at Slim's heart. "Say goodbye, Marshal."

BLAM!

Tom's hand ached...and Wichita was still standing. Suddenly it registered to Tom that not only did his hand ache, but also his gun had been shot straight out of it!

"Wha—?"

"Hello, 'One-Eyed,'" whispered Deputy Knapp, emerging from the brush with a smoking firearm.

"You like to cut these things close don't you, Knapp?" Slim observed. Tom Carson just stood his ground in wide-mouthed surprise.

"You didn't think I'd come out here alone, did you?" Slim asked Tom.

"I had...no idea..." he managed to say.

"Well, then you've learned two things today," Slim said. "One, God is *never* going to stop loving you." Slim tipped his hat to the criminal as Deputy Knapp tied Tom's wrists together.

"And number two?" Tom asked.

Knapp tapped the words on Carson's chest, "Never—*never*—underestimate a marshal!"

*Romans 3:23,10:9-10; John 3:16

THE STUMBLING BOTTLE

9

Shane realized that sometimes people
go out of their way to stumble.

I may not be the oldest and smartest kid in Eagle Grove,
but I know when to obey.

I read my Bible every morning to learn more about
obedience. My sister Shauna reads hers, too. Sometimes we
like to see who can memorize a Bible verse the fastest.

"Shane," she'll say, "I'll race you on 1 Peter 2:8!"

When I agree, we both open our Bibles to 1 Peter, read
the verse over and over until one of us shouts, *"Got it!"*
and closes the book. Then we both repeat the verse aloud—
and if one of us can't say the whole thing word-for-word,
we have to make the other's bed. I've become an expert at
bed-making.

But as I was saying, I've learned that you have to do more than just remember what the Bible says...you have to obey it. I learned that lesson last week.

I was walking home from school when I saw a bottle lying on the porch of the town saloon. Normally I just pass the saloon. I'm 11 years old and I know better than to go near that place. But the bottle was lying in front of the two-way door. I just knew that if someone came running out, they would stumble over the bottle and go flying headfirst onto the hard, dusty road.

So I walked over to move the bottle to a safer place.

To my surprise, the bottle was heavy and unopened. It was the kind that some of the grown-ups drink from—and Wichita Slim once told me that even adults shouldn't drink it. It must be pretty nasty.

You can imagine my surprise when a teenager I didn't know very well yanked the bottle out of my hands.

"What'd you find here?" he asked. I told him I was just moving the bottle so no one would get hurt. He pulled his cowboy hat down over his forehead.

"Want some?" he asked with a crooked smile.

Want some?! I thought. *You've got to be kidding! Not for anything!*

"Not really," I said politely.

He actually laughed and popped out the cork with a piece of rough wood. My eyes got as big as meatballs. He put the bottle to his lips and drank a little. He shook his head.

"This stuff'll make you a man," he promised. He wiped his lips with the back of his hand and then drank another gulp. I don't know why I didn't just run away. I guess I should have, but I'd never seen anybody be *that* stupid.

He put his arm around my shoulders and gazed into the sun.

"See, kid," he said, "today is the perfect day to become a man. This is good stuff. I know because my dad brings some home every night. I'm able to sneak some off without his knowing all the time."

I wrinkled my nose at his breath.

"In fact, if you like, you can come over and be a drinkin' partner with me. How'd you like that—having a friend in the 10th grade?"

He was being so nice, I actually began to feel bad for not taking a sip. After all, it *would* be just *one* little taste...

He handed me the bottle. It sure did smell bad.

"Got it?" he asked.

I couldn't believe it. When he said that, he sounded just like my sister earlier that morning—when she challenged me on 1 Peter 2:8.

I looked at my new friend and quoted it, "They stumble because they do not obey what God says...."

He looked at me funny.

"You gonna drink up or not?" he asked.

That's when I realized I couldn't just memorize the Word— I had to obey it, too. I turned the bottle upside down, pouring the contents all over the ground.

"No—I'm not gonna 'drink up,'" I said as the brew splashed and foamed on the dirt. "I'm stronger than that. First John 4:4 says, 'Greater is he that is in [me], than he that is in the world!'"

"What's got into you, partner?" he asked, forcefully grabbing the now-empty bottle and peering into it.

"The Holy Spirit," I responded. "Ephesians 5:18 says, 'Do not be drunk with wine. That will ruin you spiritually.

But be filled with the Spirit.'"

He looked at me, dazed, and didn't say anything else. He just threw the bottle aside and ran off. The bottle rolled along the porch planks and came to stop in front of the two-way door again.

I walked over, picked it up and threw it in the trash...but I realized something. Fact is, people who don't obey the Word will stumble over bottles like that regardless— whether it's lying on the ground or held in their hand. They'll still stumble.

But God has given me His Word and I'm going to obey it. And I know as I do, He will help keep me from stumbling. Besides, who knows...maybe I'll be able to help some other people empty their bottles—before they go flying headfirst onto a hard, dusty road.

10

**When it came to taking tests,
what Luis didn't like was the peer pressure.**

"Luis!"

Discreetly, Luis looked up from his test in the direction of the harsh whisper. It was Pete, sitting in front of him and to the left. Luis arched his eyebrows as if to ask, "What? We're taking a test!"

Pete looked at the teacher at the front of the classroom, who was leafing through some papers. Then he looked back to Luis and whispered, "What's the answer to number 12?"

This is what Luis disliked the most about tests. It wasn't the studying. It wasn't taking the test. It wasn't wondering what his grade would be. It was having to keep answers from his friends.

"I can't tell you," Luis whispered back. "It's not right." The girl sitting in front of Luis sneezed. The teacher looked up. Luis and Pete looked down. Luis began to work again.

"I'll tell you what's not right," Pete whispered a moment later. "It's not right that I might fail this test and have to take ninth grade over for the *third* time."

"Shhh!" shushed the girl in front of Luis. The teacher looked up again. Luis and Pete looked down again. Luis returned to work again.

Without warning, a scrap of folded paper landed squarely on top of Luis' head. With a roll of his eyes, Luis discreetly picked it off and unfolded it. Written on it in scraggly handwriting were the words, "WHAT IS THE ANSER TO #12?" Luis drew a small "W" between the "S" and "E," to spell "ANSWER" correctly. He wadded up the paper and threw it back at Pete. A moment later, Pete whispered under his breath, "Thanks for the spelling lesson, Luis."

DING! DING! DING! DING! DING! The teacher rang a bell.

"OK, class," she said. "Turn your tests in to me on your way out." Luis quickly circled the answer to the last question and slung his deerskin backpack over his shoulder. He handed the teacher his paper and walked out the door. Quietly, he thanked God that the peer pressure of cheating was relieved.

Soon after, Pete came out of the classroom and caught up with Luis.

"Luis!" he shouted, only a step behind him. "I thought we were friends."

Luis shook his head and stopped on the edge of the school lawn. "We are," he said. "That's why I didn't give you the answer."

"So because we're friends, you won't help me?"

"Because we're friends, I *did* help you," Luis countered. "I wouldn't let you cheat."

"Well, it's too late for that."

"What does that mean?"

Pete pulled a crumpled piece of paper from his pocket. He unfolded it and proudly revealed the answers to the test they just took. Luis' mouth dropped open.

"Why did you ask me for the answers if you already had them?" he asked.

Pete pointed to the crumpled paper. "I wrote so small, I couldn't read what I wrote for number 12," he answered. Luis huffed.

"You have to tell Teacher," he said, grabbing Pete and pulling him to the schoolhouse. "It's not right to cheat. And Galatians 6:7 says you can't cheat God—whatever you do will come back to you."

"Are you telling me *you* wouldn't cheat if you didn't study?"

Luis stopped just outside the schoolhouse door.

"That's right. I wouldn't cheat. Through Jesus, I'm stronger than that." The boys fell silent for a moment.

"Boys," a sweet voice startled them.

"Teacher!" Pete said with a wide, toothy smile as he pushed the crumpled cheat-sheet into his pants pocket. "Good test," he said enthusiastically. "Real hard."

"You earned a 90 percent, Pete," she replied. "I'm very proud of you."

Luis' eyes pierced Pete's, and Pete's stomach gurgled from uneasiness.

"You boys run home now," she said and walked back indoors.

"You've gotta tell her," Luis whispered. Pete stayed silent for a long moment.

"Wait, Teacher!" he suddenly shouted. His teacher quickly turned around and came back outside. "Yes?" she inquired.

"I'm sorry," he said, pulling the cheat-sheet out of his pocket. "I cheated."

The teacher's face dropped in disappointment and she took the tiny scrap from his hands. "Pete...we'll talk about this tomorrow morning," she said sternly, never taking her eyes off him. Briskly, she walked back into the building.

"Thanks a lot," Pete said sarcastically to Luis.

"What made you change your mind?" Luis asked his friend.

"Peer pressure, I guess," he said. "It works both ways, you know."

"Well, you did the right thing," Luis said. "It never pays to cheat. I'm just glad I could be a real friend like the Bible says—one that sharpens my friends."*

Pete nodded. "I know you're right. Thanks. Really."

Luis shook Pete's hand playfully. "Don't mention it," he said. And the two boys walked home together in silence.

*Proverbs 27:17ß

DEPUTY WORRYWART

11

**Knapp was ready to toss in his badge...
until he realized he could toss in his worries instead.**

"Woe is me," Deputy Knapp said walking into the marshal's office. Wichita Slim got up from his chair and walked over to shake his deputy's hand. When their palms met, Wichita let out a yelp and yanked his hand back.

"Sorry, Marshal," Roy Knapp said. He opened his hand to reveal his deputy's badge—with six pointy corners. Each one glistened in the summer afternoon sunlight that was shining through the window. He handed his badge over to Slim...carefully this time.

"Why aren't you wearing your badge, Deputy?" Slim asked. "Is it broken?"

"No, it's not broken...but my heart is," Knapp said,

shutting his eyes tightly and letting his chin quiver. Slim's face crinkled up and then his expression was broken by a smile. He knew Knapp was sometimes a little overdramatic.

"Knapp, is something troubling you?" he asked, sitting back down behind his desk. Knapp tossed his badge on the wooden surface. It landed with a hollow clink.

"I'm in a world of trouble," Knapp admitted, shaking his head. "I'm gonna have to set aside my duties until I get outta this mess. You and Deputy Rigler will just have to take care of the town by yourselves for a while."

Wichita stood back up and leaned over his desk. He peered into Knapp's watery, brown eyes. "What sort of trouble are you in, Roy?"

"Oh, it's nothin' illegal, Marshal," Knapp said. "It's just that...well...I'm a *worrywart,* OK?" He turned around, embarrassed. Slim was noticeably taken aback.

"A *worrywart?*" The marshal asked, wincing. "Knapp, if it's all right, I'd rather just call you a *deputy.*"

"Fine. I'm *Deputy Worrywart.*"

"Just *Deputy,*" Slim said, picking up the deputy's badge for emphasis. He sat down again. For a moment, neither lawman said anything. Then Wichita broke the silence.

"So you find yourself worrying a lot?"

"Yeah. I'm always worrying," Knapp responded, pacing the floor. "I worry that somebody might shoot me when I'm not looking...I worry that somebody might shoot me when I *am* looking...I worry that I'll forget to feed my horse...I worry about what might happen tomorrow...I worry about what people think of me when I walk by...I—"

"I get the picture," Slim interjected. "That *is* a load of worries."

"Yep." Knapp sighed. He felt like crumbling to the floor.

"I'm a worrywart."

That word made Wichita grimace again. "What does God say about you being a...about you worrying?"

Knapp scratched his head. That question got his attention. "You know, I just don't know. Sure, I've prayed about it— but God hasn't said a thing to me."

THUMP! Wichita tossed his Bible onto the desk. "I reckon God has said a lot more than you think."

"You mean in there?" Knapp said, pointing to the Bible.

"Yep." Slim picked up the Bible. "Knapp, this Bible is God's Word to you and me. Any answer we need for life can be found in here—it's a lamp for our feet and a light for our way."*

"So what does God say about my worrying?" Knapp asked, twisting his lips. Slim opened his Bible to 1 Peter 5:7. He turned it around so Knapp could read it.

"'Give all your worries to him, because he cares for you'—wow!" Knapp's eyes became the size of silver dollars. "I didn't know God said He'd take my worries!"

"Now it's up to you to *take God at His Word*," Slim added.

"How do I do that?" Roy asked.

"By faith," the marshal responded. "You need to believe that what He said is true—that you *can* give your worries to Him. Then you must actually give them to Him by believing what He said."

Knapp stared at the deputy badge as Wichita spun it around on his palm.

"Won't God just take my worries without me having to do anything?"

Slim chuckled. "God's given you His promise, but you have to act on it." He got up, walked to the window and pointed to his horse. "Knapp, say I told you that you could have my horse. Now that's great—but if you don't go saddle it up and start riding, what I said won't change the way you go home tonight."

"I think I understand," Knapp admitted. "So I have to do more than just read God's Word. I have to listen to it and do what it says with faith in God."

Slim pointed his finger at Knapp now. "You got it," he said. Relief flooded over Knapp's face.

"All right! I *can* get rid of all these worries!" Knapp shouted. "I'm going to go pray right now and let God have them all—because He said to in His Word." He headed toward the door, but then stopped and turned around.

"Oops, I almost forgot my badge," he said. Wichita held it out to him.

"Are you sure, Deputy? You're going to stop worrying?"

"No more *Deputy Worrywart!*" Roy Knapp said with a smile as he snatched the badge out of the marshal's hand. "You've got *my* word...because I've got God's!"

With that, he turned around, exited and let the door shut behind him. Slim let out a short laugh and closed his Bible. "Thank the Lord," he whispered. When he looked out the window, he saw Knapp riding away carefree.

*Psalm 119:105

Who's Afraid of

The Dark?

12

**Shauna knew she shouldn't have been out so late...
and now the darkness was closing in.**

My brother's the one with the big imagination. Not me.
I know when something *isn't* imaginary—like when I'm
being followed.

When I first saw it behind me, it was big, dark
and...well, that's about it. But I'm sure it was after me. Now,
my brother sometimes thinks there are *monsters* after him,
but I don't believe in monsters. I always say, "Shane, go
back to sleep. There's nothing to be scared about." He just
says, "You'd be scared if a huge, shadowy monster was
after you, Shauna." But I've never believed in such things.

Until tonight.

Tonight I knew there was something after me.

Who's afraid of the dark? Well, I've been told all my life that I don't have to be. But earlier tonight I was. Because— I'm telling you the truth—*The Dark* was following me.

Actually, it was chasing me. No matter where I went, there it was, right on my heels. Now, I knew I'd be in big trouble if Joy (the nice lady I live with) knew I was outside this late. I'm only 7 1/2 years old and I should have had an adult with me. But 15 minutes earlier when I was at a friend's house, I noticed the sun was nearly down. So, I just decided I'd run home quick before it got too late.

Well, the sun didn't waste any time going down...and it got too late.

So there I was, still five minutes from home and *The Dark* was closing in. This was not my idea of fun.

Thump-thump! Thump-thump! Thump-thump!

That's it! I heard it! *The Dark* was coming after me!

Naturally, I did what any sensible kid would do in this situation. I took off running! I looked back over my shoulder, but it was still gaining on me. How could I ever outrun—

SMACK!

Oh, no! *I ran into it!* And it hurt! I must have heard its echoes between the buildings and thought it was behind me...when it was really in front of me!

"Leave me alone!" I screamed, hitting *The Dark* with all my might. "I'm just a nice little red-haired girl!"

"Shauna Decker?" It answered back. I stopped hitting it for a moment... It knew my name?

"Shauna—are you all right?"

I knew that voice. And it wasn't *The Dark*. It was the marshal.

"Wichita Slim?!" I asked as my eyes began to get used to seeing in the night. There he was on top of his horse—the one I was hitting. But what a relief! I may be in trouble, but better that than left alone with *The Dark!*

The marshal hopped off his horse and asked me what I was doing out in the dark. I told him I was running from it.

"You shouldn't be out so late," he said sternly. But then he kneeled down and looked into my wide eyes. He asked, "Are you afraid of the dark, Shauna?"

"Not as much as my brother is," I responded, after gulping.

"Let me show you something."

Wichita Slim reached into his jacket and pulled out a little stick. Then he scraped it on his boot and immediately a brilliant white light filled the space between us. I jumped back a little as the flame filled my eyesight and then I looked around me. Wherever the marshal held the match, the darkness ran away—as fast as it could.

"The Dark is afraid of the light!" I cheered.

"That's right," the Marshal said. "And God says in His Word that *you're* the light that gives light to the world."

"I'm light?" I asked.

"Yes, ma'am. And when you do good things, the things of God, you shine so bright that *The Dark* can't live in other people's lives."*

That's when I realized that even though I felt like I was being chased by *The Dark,* some people actually *live* in *The Dark*—because they don't know Jesus. That's why it's important for me to shine...so that others can see Jesus in me. Sure, *The Dark* may be all around, but with Jesus in my life, I can shine right in the middle of it—and it has to run away.

"So there's no reason to be afraid when God's with me," I said to the marshal. He agreed and lifted me up on his horse to take me home. Well, a few minutes later, Joy was thrilled to see me safe and told me we'd talk tomorrow.

That was an hour ago. Now, I'm all tucked in, safe and sound, and ready to go to sleep. And I'm keeping that little match right beside my bed to remind me what I learned tonight.

So who's afraid of *The Dark?* Not me. Because with Jesus on my side, *The Dark* is the one who ends up running.

*Matthew 5:14-16

The Impatient PATIENT

13

**Clara didn't understand how talking about
tomatoes would make her flu go away...**

Joy, the town's one and only nurse, was taking Clara's
temperature when Dr. Grant, the town's one and only
doctor, entered the room.

"So who do we have here?" Dr. Grant asked the nurse.
She squeezed Clara's warm hand.

"This is Clara Rigler, the deputy's daughter," Joy said.
"She's 10 and she's not feeling very well this afternoon."

"Is that true?" the large, dark-skinned doctor asked Clara.

"Yep, I turned 10 last June," Clara responded. The
doctor laughed.

"No, I mean is it true that you're not feeling well?"

"That's true, too," she said. So with great care, the

doctor checked her ears and her eyes. Then he made her say, "Aaaah," and he checked her throat.

"Well, Clara," Dr. Grant pronounced after his checkup. "It seems you have a case of the common flu."

"So how can I get rid of it?" Clara wondered aloud. Her voice was a little raspy and she looked tired. The doctor smiled.

"Well, someday we may have the cure," he said. "But for now, all you can do is ride it out."

"But I want to get rid of it *now!*" Clara insisted, followed by a cough.

"We'll believe God for your healing," Joy interjected. "But if you want to live in *continual* health, you'll have to plant some seeds."

Clara's eyebrows scrunched together and dove toward her nose. *Continually* healthy? she thought. That sounded pretty good compared to having the flu. "What do you mean?" she finally asked.

Dr. Grant moved over to the window and peered outside. "C'mere," he said, motioning to Clara. Obediently, she slid off the soft bench and walked over to the doctor. He was pointing out the window now. Clara followed the path of his index finger and saw a small garden in the distance.

"You see that tomato plant out there?" he asked. Clara nodded. It was a tall, green plant in the center of the garden. It had leaves from top to bottom and hanging from several branches were plump, red tomatoes. Just seeing them made Clara's mouth water.

"That tomato plant used to be *this*," Dr. Grant said. Then he opened the hand he was pointing with. In the center of his palm was a tiny, pointed seed—as small as a pebble. Clara looked out the window again at the plant. She wondered how it was possible that the big plant and the tiny seed used to be the exact same thing.

"The difference," Nurse Joy replied, reading the question on Clara's face, "is that one seed was planted, watered and received a lot of care. The other was left alone and never even put into the ground."

Wow, Clara thought. Then she shook her head and asked, "But what does planting *tomatoes* have to do with getting rid of my flu?"

Joy picked up a Bible from a nearby table.

"God's Word is like this seed," she said, pointing to the seed in Dr. Grant's hand. "And it can grow to create a harvest of health in your life. But first you have to plant it in your heart."*

Clara scratched her head. "How do I do that?"

"By reading and speaking the promises God wrote to you in the Bible," Dr. Grant responded. "For instance, you could say 1 Peter 2:24—'We are healed because of his wounds.' You can even make it personal by saying, '*I* am healed because of Jesus' wounds.'"*

"OK!" Clara said excitedly. She felt like she was finally getting somewhere. "Will you write that down for me? I'm ready to say it and be healed!"

"Not so fast," Joy said, brushing back a strand of Clara's blonde hair. "It takes time for a seed to grow. And you have to water it, give it sunlight and take care of it."

Clara started tapping her foot. "So how do I do *that* for the seed of God's Word in my heart?"

"By continuing to read the Bible and speaking God's promises aloud in faith," Dr. Grant said.

"And also by praying and going to a church where they'll water your seed by teaching you how to use your faith," Joy added. "You have to keep that seed growing and not let any seeds of doubt get in. You have to keep believing God."

Clara thought about it for a moment.

"Actually, that sounds pretty simple," she said.

"It *is* simple," Joy replied, "because God wants His kids healthy."

"And if you'll start planting God's Word into your heart today, it may be a while before I see you again," the doctor said with a wink.

Clara looked at the seed and the Bible intently.

"I'll do it!" she said. "I want to get a harvest of health in my life so I don't get this nasty, old flu again."

With her mind made up, Clara grabbed the Bible and the tomato seed and headed for the door. "Thank you, doctor, for the prescription," she said, referring to the Bible. "I'll plant the seed of God's Word in my heart, and I'll be well in no time."

Dr. Grant winked again and Joy smiled wide. "I believe you will," he said. "And pray over your medicine as well, that it would bless your body and have no side effects."

Clara giggled. Then she held up the seed. "And I'll plant *this* seed right away, too," she said. "It can help remind me to keep sowing seeds even when I'm well."

With that, she turned around, closed the office door and headed home. As she walked, she began speaking God's promises, believing she received as she spoke...and by the time she reached her front door, she was already beginning to feel better.

*Mark 4:26-29; Proverbs 4:20-22

14

**Clara discovered that believing for a baby brother
was the same as seeing him by faith.**

Clara's bottom lip protruded, displaying her obvious discontentment. In one hand, she spun around a dull, red bow that had been attached to one of her Christmas presents that morning. A wisp of blond hair dropped down in front of her face and tickled the knuckles on her other hand that was propped underneath her chin. Clara brushed the wisp away.

The crisp, early afternoon air chilled her cheeks bright red, but she kept the rest of herself warm in a double-layered winter coat lined with soft fur—a Christmas present from her Indian friends, Rising Sun and Water Dancer. But the cold breath of the wind wasn't what chilled Clara to the bone. It was the hope that had frozen inside her...the hope that she wanted to thaw again, but didn't know how.

Clara heard the front door creak open, but didn't have to turn around to know it was her dad, Deputy Joel Rigler. His heavy footsteps gave him away. She turned her head and offered a weak smile to the red-haired man as he sat down beside her.

"Brrrrr! It's cold out here!" He folded his arms over his chest and gave a fake shiver. Clara smiled. "So what on earth would make my 10-year-old daughter sit outside in the cold during such a wonderful day."

Clara shrugged her shoulders. Mr. Rigler scratched his head and then pulled on his long, red mustache.

"Claire," he prodded, using her nickname, "you can tell me—I'm your dad, remember?" Clara nodded. They were both quiet for a long moment.

"It's about something I wanted for Christmas," she finally said. "But I'm not being selfish...in fact, it's not even something for me. It's something I wanted for you and Mom."

Joel Rigler's big, ruddy eyebrows bobbed up and down. "Something for me and Mom?" he asked. "Honey, we received more than we could have hoped for this Christmas. God has really blessed us all."

"There's *one* thing you didn't get," Clara said. Her dad's mouth opened silently as he suddenly caught on to what his daughter was referring to. Only a few seconds passed before Clara acknowledged it herself.

"You and Mom said that you've been wanting to have another baby for a couple years now...but the doctor said it may not be possible. So that's what I wanted more than anything this Christmas. I wanted Mom to find out she was going to have another baby—a baby boy."

Clara thumped her chin back down on her palm. Deputy Rigler put his arm around her.

"Sweetheart, do you remember the Christmas story?" he asked. Clara nodded. "In Luke 2:13-14, it says that a whole group of angels appeared to some shepherds when Jesus was born. The Bible says, 'All the angels were praising God, saying: "Glory to God in the highest, And on earth peace, goodwill toward men!"'*

"Yeah, I remember that," Clara admitted. "But what does that have to do with Mom having a baby?"

"Well," Rigler said, smiling big, "here's something you may have never thought about: God sent the angels to say those words—but Jesus was only an infant. He hadn't performed one miracle yet. He hadn't resisted one temptation yet. And he certainly hadn't died on the cross and rose again. Still, the angels were declaring peace between God and people."

"So why would God say there was peace between God and people if it hadn't happened yet?" Clara wondered.

"He was using *faith*," Rigler answered. "Romans 4:17 says God 'calls those things which do not exist as though they did.' God had His faith set on what Jesus would do. As far as He was concerned, it was already done. And you know what? Because of God's faith and love, everything turned out perfectly."*

Clara turned to her father. "You know what, Dad? If that's the way God uses His faith, that's the way I want to use mine, too. I may not see my baby brother yet, but I'm going to keep believing that he's going to come. By faith, I can see him already."

"Well, your mother and I are agreeing with you, so Amen," Rigler punctuated with a nod. "And with faith, we'll be able to celebrate the joy of Christmas all year long."

Suddenly, Clara pushed herself up.

"Where you going?" her dad asked with a smile.

"Inside," his daughter responded casually. "I'm ready to celebrate Christmas the way it should be celebrated. I'm going to thank God for everything I received...and everything that's still to come."

Clara giggled aloud and her father followed her into the warm house.

The New King James Version

TOO MUCH TIME WITH THE FROGS

15

**Luis was surprised to discover that, without realizing it,
he'd been spending too much time with the frogs.**

"Ribbit!"

The riverbank was soft and warm, inviting to the lively
outdoor creatures. Frogs, fat bumblebees and a salamander
or two hopped, fluttered and crawled here and there,
oblivious to the stationary team sitting on the bank with
wooden fishing poles in hand.

Billy Bob Statler and his teenage, hired help and friend,
Luis Sanchez, were relaxing in wait for a grand dinner
catch. The sun glistened off the slowly rolling water that
pulled their lines, hooks and bait with its current.

The day was beautiful and refreshing. Luis sniffed
loudly. Billy Bob looked at him with his lips curled.

"You know that's the seventeenth time you've sniffed since we ate lunch?" Billy Bob questioned. The statement made Luis laugh. He always appreciated Billy Bob's openness, because he always knew exactly what he was thinking.

"Yeah, I know. I'm sorry," Luis said with a smile. "It's just this stupid cold. I've been trying to shake it for three weeks now. Who ever heard of someone getting a cold in the summertime?"

"You've been sniffing for three weeks?"

"And coughing sometimes—and feeling all stuffed up. I've been miserable; it just won't leave. I've tried sleeping for 24 hours straight, eating raw eggs and standing on my head with an onion slice on my nose."

Billy Bob Statler laughed. "Well, that certainly explains why you've been miserable..."

Luis nodded and sniffed again.

"Sounds like you've been spending too much time with the frogs," Statler said, nodding his head toward a hopping, green amphibian.

"Frogs?!" Luis shouted, reeling in disgust. "I don't follow you, B.B."

Billy Bob shoved his fishing pole into the earth and twisted it until it was stuck in strong. "Story time," he announced, turning to fully face Luis. Before speaking, he brushed both sides of his red beard once with his hand, a familiar gesture he made whenever he had something to say.

"Thousands of years ago, an Egyptian Pharaoh had a problem just like yours," he told Luis.

Luis sniffed again. "An Egyptian Pharaoh had the sniffles?"

Statler smiled. "No, he had the frogs."

"Come again?"

"You see, he was in a dispute with God because he

wouldn't let the Israelites out of slavery. But God wanted them out. So, one morning he awoke to find his country swarming with frogs."*

Luis grimaced. "Eww! Stinky, slimy, croaking, warty frogs?"

"Hopping all over the place. There were big, old frogs in their beds, on their tables, in their ovens; little, bitty frogs in their bread dough, in their drinking water, in their hair..."

Luis put up his hands. "I get the picture."

"Anyway," Statler continued, "after letting Pharaoh spend a while with the frogs, God sent in His man Moses to request, 'Please set the time that I should pray for the frogs to leave you and your houses.' And do you know what Pharaoh's answer was?"

"The sooner the better!" Luis said enthusiastically.

"Nope. He said, 'Tomorrow.'"

Luis' mouth dropped open in shock and he nearly dropped his fishing pole. Down the riverbank, a frog croaked. "Are you telling me he was willing to spend the rest of the day—and all night—with those frogs?! Why in the world would he wait until 'tomorrow'?"

"Probably for the same reason people always wait until tomorrow to receive what they need—whether it be salvation, help or...healing, Luis."

The words smacked Luis like a wayward horseshoe—hitting him before he even knew they were coming.

"Here's what's interesting," Billy Bob continued. "When Moses asked that question and Pharaoh answered, 'Tomorrow,' Moses said, 'All right. Let it be done just as you've said.' It was Pharaoh's own words that led him to spending more time with those frogs—and his decision."

Luis looked at the frog on the riverbank and sniffed. "But I can tell you I've decided I don't want the sniffles!"

"What have you been saying?"

"Only that they won't go away. And that I've had them for three weeks and can't shake them. And...oops...I've been saying the wrong things, haven't I?"

"You need to speak the real truth—God's Word—instead, friend."

"You're right. I don't wanna live with these frogs one more night! I'm going to choose to believe God's Word. First Peter 2:24 says I am healed because of Jesus' wounds! And that's what you're going to hear coming out of my mouth from now on!"

"All right!" Statler shouted in agreement as he yanked his fishing pole out of the ground. The frog at the bottom of the bank slipped into the water and disappeared.

"Well, I do believe you've caught on," Billy Bob said with a smile.

"Yep. I've finally decided I don't want to spend any more time with the frogs."

"Well, yes...but I mean I do believe you've caught on, Luis—to tonight's dinner."

Luis suddenly realized his fishing pole was bent down at the top and his line was taut.

"All right!" he shouted. And together, the two friends pulled in a record-sized catch.

*Exodus 8

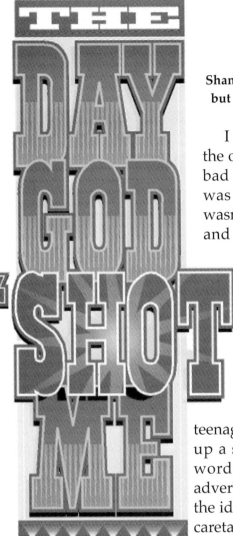

THE DAY GOD 'SHOT' ME

16

**Shane knew cussing was wrong...
but he just had to try it anyway.**

I cussed for the first time the other day. I did it. I said a bad word—and I knew it was bad when I said it. It wasn't like when I was five and said a bad word by accident. This time I knew what I was saying...and I said it anyway. I was curious. Besides, as an 11-year-old in a small town, I wanted everyone to see how mature I was. I have a teenage cousin who can "cuss up a storm." He uses cuss words like adjectives and adverbs—that's where I got the idea. I know Miss Joy, my caretaker, says cussing shows lack of creativity. But it is a mature-*sounding* lack of creativity anyway.

So, there I was in the middle of the street, when a horse-drawn wagon rolled by. One of those big, wooden wheels slapped into a puddle of thick mud and—you guessed it—I got sloshed from the head down. I could feel my blood boil. I could feel my fists tighten. I let go of all restraint and LET IT OUT!

"FILTH!" I shouted. (Well, OK, that's not *exactly* what I said, but I think you get the idea.)

I tell you, everyone within a square mile froze in their tracks, turned in my direction and dropped their mouths. I smiled. Then I frowned.

I don't know any way to explain it other than to say my mouth tasted bad—like I'd just taken a bite of chalk or licked a bar of soap. But that wasn't all. When I said that word, it felt like something moved into my thinking—some kind of outlaw that warned if I continued, he would gradually take over. I know that may sound strange, but that's what it felt like.

"You're at a crossroad, son," a deep voice said from behind me. I twirled around and came face to face with Wichita Slim. Talk about being embarrassed. He was kneeling beside his horse, looking me straight in the eye. I gulped.

The marshal reached to his side and pulled out his weapon, pointing it straight at me—a black, leather, palm-sized Bible. And it was fully loaded.

He opened it up, cocking back the hammer. Then he pulled the trigger.

"Ephesians 4:17-19 talks about people who harden their hearts and lose their sensitivity. It says they give themselves over to lasciviousness—and then they can't stop...they want more and more."

The shot stopped short of piercing my heart.

"I would never give myself over to laseeousess...

er...lassivus...er...you know. I'd never do that," I promised.

Wichita Slim didn't drop his gaze. "Son, do you know what lasciviousness is?"

I paused. I had made it a rule to never learn about anything I couldn't pronounce. Like isthmus. Who came up with that word, anyway? Of course I didn't know what lasciviousness was. I shook my head no.

"Lasciviousness," the marshal explained, "means to have no restraint. It means just letting go whenever, with whatever."

The shot went straight through me and exploded on the inside. "Like I just did," I admitted.

The marshal nodded. "It starts out as just a few seemingly innocent thoughts," he explained. "But then they grow and grow until they turn into some serious sin. You first think, 'Aw, I'm just curious.' Then...finally...you do what you know you shouldn't. Then you do it again. Then again."

"Without restraint," I pieced together.

I realized right then and there I had a choice: Was I going to let that spiritual outlaw, Satan, have me do his bidding? Would his strategy work on me? Would I give him control? *Or* would I decide to obey God in even little things like this? Would I choose not to cuss, and follow Him one step at a time instead?

Marshal Slim didn't say anything else. In fact, by the time I was about to respond, he was already riding away on his horse. The gawking townspeople were back about their business, too. The choice was up to me and me alone.

I reached up and placed my hand over my heart. His Word had shot me to the core. He was teaching me and I made my decision—*I was going to listen.*

The bullet He sent into my heart remained...only now it felt like it was...healing. Perhaps it had been all along.

Suddenly, I realized that something *else* had happened when I made that decision to never cuss again. I had grown. Yep, ironically, I had become more mature. Which, as you might remember, was what I had wanted all along.

17

**Clara wanted to get God
the perfect present for Christmas...**

It was Sunday afternoon and Clara sat on a bench outside the Eagle Grove General Store. Her chin was in her hand and her elbow rested in her lap as she sulked. It was chilly, but Clara didn't care. *That* was the least of her concerns.

All the 10-year-old wanted this mid-December day was an idea for a gift—a *good* gift that someone would be proud to receive. This was especially important to Clara...because the one she wanted to give a gift to was God.

"God has done so many good things for me," she had told her mother. "I want to do something for Him. What kind of gift would He like?"

Clara's mother fell speechless. "Well...I don't know,

Clara...what doesn't God already have?"

Clara bit her lip, then decided she would make Him a gift. She found some paper and scissors and clipped together a little paper boat with a pop-up sail. But when she finished her project and inspected it, she was less than thrilled. The bottom of the boat wasn't entirely straight, and when she put it in water, it sank.

"It's just not *perfect*," Clara stated. "It just won't do!"

Not long after the soggy sailboat ended up in the trash, Clara set out for the General Store with six coins she had saved.

Mr. Johnson met her inside.

"I need to find something for someone who has everything," Clara explained.

Mr. Johnson didn't skip a beat. He brought Clara right over to a towering display.

"*This*," he shouted, "is the Apple Slicer 2200! It's the newest item of the season—came all the way from New York City! All you do is put an apple in here." Mr. Johnson placed an apple into the machine's small, iron clamp. "Then you slide this lever, push this button and turn the crank three times. Ta-daaaaa!"

As Mr. Johnson sang, the apple popped under pressure and juice and mush splattered onto the table.

"Instant apple mush," Clara concluded.

Mr. Johnson fiddled with the machine, mumbling something about getting his money back.

Clara sighed. "No thanks, Mr. Johnson," she said. "I'll keep looking."

When Clara left the store, she was fresh out of ideas. She toppled down onto the bench outside, where she sat sulking for nearly a half-hour.

Clomp! Clomp! Clomp! Clomp!

Clara smiled when she heard the horse's trot. Somehow, she knew the trot of her daddy's horse from any other in town.

Deputy Rigler tied up his horse, marched up the General Store's steps and sat down beside his daughter. He gave her a kiss on the forehead and put his arm around her.

"Well, if it isn't my one-and-only Clara," he announced. "What ever is the matter?"

Clara told her dad how she wanted to give God a present—a special present—for Christmas, but couldn't find the perfect gift. She tried to make one, she tried to buy one, but nothing was just right.

"That's a tough one," Deputy Rigler remarked. "John 3:16 says God has given us the greatest gift of all—His Son, Jesus. He came to earth and died in our place so we could live in victory and be with Him forever. But what on earth could we possibly give Him in return?"

Clara twisted a lock of her blond hair on her forefinger. "I know it," she muttered.

A long moment passed when, suddenly, Clara's blue eyes opened wide as a thought occurred to her.

"Daddy—that's it!" she exclaimed.

"What? What's it?!"

"Well, if the greatest gift of all was a Son, wouldn't a perfect gift for God be a son or daughter?"

Deputy Rigler pursed his upper lip, making his big, red mustache rumple.

"I'm not sure if I follow, Clara."

Clara scooted to the edge of the bench so she could look straight into her father's face as she explained it to him.

"Well, God sent His Son Jesus as a gift to us. He did it because He loved us—so we could become His sons and daughters, right?"

"Right..."

"So that's what I'll give God!"

"But you're already his daughter, Clara. You're a Christian."

"Right! But if I tell someone else about Him, they might become a Christian, too!"

Deputy Rigler pondered Clara's idea for a moment and then said, "You know, Clara, I think that's a great idea."

"And the best thing is," Clara said, "I don't have to wait until Christmas! I can share Jesus with others all year 'round, so God can receive sons and daughters anytime!"

Deputy Rigler slapped his knees in agreement and stood up. "It looks like your problem is solved," he said to Clara. "Now you just have to go plant seeds of love by what you say and how you live."

Clara nodded and waved as her daddy rode away.

With a squeal, she ran off the porch and headed to the school playground where she knew many of her friends would be. She was ready to give to God. And she wasn't going to just give Him any old thing like a soggy paper boat or an apple musher. No, He was her Heavenly Father. And He deserved the perfect gift.

Back on Track

18

**When the train got off track,
Shane decided not to go with it.**

You heard about the time One-Eyed Tom Carson hijacked the 10:40 train coming out of Wichita? Yeah, it's the one that Marshal Slim got back on track with faith in God and a good aim. Well, I was *on* that train.

Miss Soh and I were in the third passenger car and everything was just fine. I was helping Miss Soh deliver some medicine to a town an hour away. We were only about fifteen minutes into our trip when it happened.

A screeching sound pricked my ears. It made a shiver crawl down my spine. I jumped from Miss Soh's side and pressed my nose to the window. My stomach sank when I saw One-Eyed Tom Carson—scoundrel of scoundrels—

jumping onto the train, gun drawn. He had thrown the switch and forced us onto a different track—one that gave him the advantage.

"What's wrong?" Miss Soh asked sweetly. I shook my head. I didn't want to worry her. I wanted to be brave. I wanted to be strong. I wanted to do *something,* but we were being hijacked—and most likely robbed. The thought made me tense.

I looked down at the box of medicine Miss Soh had under her folded hands. Wouldn't it be nice if someone invented "courage medicine" that made you fearless?

Suddenly, the voice of the Lord spoke from inside me and boldly said, *Courage comes from faith in Me.*

I gulped. He didn't say anything else. He didn't need to. I closed my eyes.

"Father God," I prayed in a whisper, "I put my faith in You. Your Word says to be strong and courageous. I won't be terrified or discouraged. I will have courage. For You are with me."*

I decided to believe. I decided to have faith.

When I opened my eyes, I couldn't help but shout! There, outside the window, I saw Wichita Slim riding alongside the train! He had come to take care of that villainous villain! He leaned toward the train, ready to grab on when—

BOOM!!

Like lightning, the locomotive picked up speed. Slim's horse instantly fell behind. I wanted to gasp. I wanted to worry. I wanted to bite my nails. If Wichita Slim couldn't get on board...*no.* I *wouldn't* worry. I kept my faith—and it stirred my courage. I didn't know what else to say, so I just shouted, "In Jesus' Name!" I got a few funny looks.

But, would you believe—I promise I'm not making this

up—Wichita's horse started running *as fast as* the train!?! It's true! Within seconds, Slim jumped onto the side of the train and climbed up top.

It wasn't long after that when Slim stopped One-Eyed Tom Carson, the train slowed down and we got back on track. The rest you know—you've heard the story. But I still wonder...if I hadn't been courageous and joined my faith with Slim's...what would have happened?

I'm glad we'll never have to find out. I'm glad God was able to use me to help save the day—all because I decided to stay on the right track.

*Joshua 1:9; Psalm 46:1

19

**With his grades falling, Luis is looking for a
plan to get them back on track.**

"YEEEOWWW!" cried 14-year-old Luis Sanchez. He
dropped the hammer and popped his throbbing thumb
into his mouth. Billy Bob Statler, Luis' friend and ranch
boss, chuckled.

"Twice in one hour," he said. "That must be some
sorta record."

Luis winced. "Nah punny," he said.

The two friends were building a barn together. The main
structure for one wall was completed. With only three more
walls to go, Statler set down the two wooden planks he just
carried over from a large pile.

"Well, look at it this way," he said, "how many more

times can you hit your thumb in one day?"

Luis inspected his thumb. "I'm not sure I wanna find out."

Statler decided to take a break. He sat down and brushed his brow with a small cloth. "What's wrong, Luis?" he asked.

Luis let out a long breath. "I'm sorry, B.B.," he said. "My mind's just not in this." Then, after a pause, "My grades aren't doing so well."

"You mean at school?"

Luis nodded. "I'm studying hard and believing God that I'll get better grades, but...It just doesn't look good right now."

"Sounds like you've lost hope."

"I've got faith."

"But it sounds like you've lost *hope.*"

"What's the difference?" Luis wondered.

"The difference," explained Statler, "is that your faith is either standing strong"—he hit a cross-section of the wall structure with his hammer—"or it's just lying there"—he pointed to the pile of wooden planks.

Luis shrugged his shoulders. "So how do I get my faith to stand strong for my schoolwork?"

Statler reached in his pocket and pulled out an old, rumpled piece of paper. He handed it to Luis. "You know what this is?" he asked.

Luis unraveled the paper. Inside, drawn in fine charcoal, was a picture of the barn they were building—with markings and notations down to the last board.

Luis' dark eyebrows shot up. "This is your plan for building this barn," he answered.

"This," Billy Bob Statler said as he grabbed the paper, "is my hope that what we're building will turn out to *be* a barn. But, Luis, if I didn't have this hope—this plan—how would

I know that all this lumber would turn out to be anything?"

Luis rubbed his thumb.

"Your faith needs to build on your hope in God," Statler said. "The Bible says faith is the *substance* of things *hoped* for—just like these beams are the *substance* of what I drew on this paper."*

"Well, my faith could build on God's promise to give me wisdom," Luis pointed out.*

"Yes! *There's* your hope," Statler said. "Put your hope in God's promise of wisdom to you."

"And then my faith will turn that hope into reality!" Luis let out a short laugh. "I don't know why I let myself get so discouraged. I'm *going* to have hope," he promised.

"Great," Billy Bob said slapping his knees with his palms. "Then let's get back to work."

"All right!" Luis said. Then, "But B.B.?"

"Yeah?"

"Is there something I can do other than hammering? I'm running out of thumbs!"

*Hebrews 11:1; James 1:5

The Trouble With Strife

20

**When strife pressures Shane,
he discovers how to apply pressure back.**

I was walking out of church and that kid—Wayne Burski—
you know, the one everyone calls "Bully," knocked my arm.

"Hey!" I shouted.

Wayne laughed. "What're you gonna do, Shane?"

Now as an 11-year-old, I've had to deal with getting
picked on before. I've got red hair, lots of freckles. Sometimes
that's all it takes. When you're a bully, *anything* can be used
to start a fight.

I just shook my head. *Why give him an inch?*

Suddenly I felt a tap on my shoulder. I nearly jumped
when I turned. There it was—staring me in the face: Strife.
It was even bigger than Wayne and looked a whole lot more

deserving of the name, "Bully."

"Psst!" Strife said. "Let him have it! Don't let him treat you like that!"

I grimaced. No chance. Wayne is *way* bigger than me and I'm not about to go head-to-head.

"No big deal," Strife answered back, as if reading my thoughts. "We can do our work later."

"What are you talking about?" I asked, giving Wayne a look out of the corner of my eye.

Strife slid in front of me, blocking my view. "What I'm saying, kid, is that I know you're small. But you can make Wayne smaller!"

I peeked over Strife's shoulder. He was right. I could. I could go home and tell my sister, Shauna, all about what a loser Wayne was. I could tell her about the awful things he's done and how he'll pick on anyone half his size. She's never met him, but I could help her make up her mind about him anyway.

Oh! And then I could go to school and tell Pete and Luis and a bunch of other kids that actually *know* Wayne! They'd see him for who he was and suddenly he wouldn't have any friends. That would teach him for picking on me.

Strife's black eyes glistened.

A chill ran down my back. I'd been told about that look. Wichita Slim told me about it. It was a proud look. And Marshal Slim said that's one of the things the Lord *hates.* Whoa.

Suddenly, the Holy Spirit shook my heart. It felt like an earthquake in my chest. I immediately remembered the verses Slim once read to me: Proverbs 6:16-19. "The Lord hates…a lying tongue, a heart that devises wicked schemes, feet that are quick to rush into evil…and a man who stirs up dissension among brothers."

The Lord hates strife.

I stared Strife back in its haughty eyes. "No," I said aloud. Strife blinked.

"I said, *no*," I repeated. "There is no way, no how, you can get me to stir up strife. I choose to walk in love."

Strife shrieked. "Ugh!" he shouted. "Don't say that word!"

"Not only will I say it, I will *do* it!" I replied with confidence. "Love *never* fails."*

Immediately, I pushed Strife out of my way. It was easier than I thought.

As I trounced forward, I saw Wayne freeze and tighten his fists. He saw the determination in my eyes and he was ready for a fight.

I smiled. "Hey, Wayne," I said. "I'm not going to get into strife with you. Instead, I'm going to pray for you each and every day. I'll be praying that you get to know God like never before. And I hope that as I do, you see His love in me."

Wayne blinked. He was speechless. I made the bully speechless! When I looked over my shoulder, Strife was nowhere to be seen. Finally, as I turned to go, Wayne got up the courage to say, "Whatever."

But that's OK. I know Wayne heard what I said. It was all over his face. And I know that my actions will make a difference. By walking in love, my sister and my friends won't think bad of him because of me. And who knows? Maybe my prayers and actions will end up changing Wayne's life for the better. I wouldn't doubt it. Because that's the other thing Slim told me: *Love never fails.*

*1 Corinthians 13:8

21

**When Shauna was accused of pride,
she examined herself with the Word.**

I heard he lived in my town, but I'd never met him. In my nine years here, I've never *wanted* to meet him. I heard he was stingy and angry and not the sort you'd want to come across in a dark alley. You can imagine my surprise then, when on the way home, I ran right into him! His face was wrinkly like a prune, his fingertips like raisins. His mouth was drawn down as if gravity had sucked away his smile.

Now I know what you're thinking: *There's no one in your town like that!* I know it! But I met him that day, as I was walking with my head held high.

He moved right in front of me and stopped, staring

down. I stopped in my tracks and looked up.

"Um… Hello. I haven't seen you around here before. What's your name?" I asked politely, my voice shaking. I imagine my blue eyes were as big as meatballs.

"I," he said slowly, "am Mr. Tradition." He pulled his hand away so I couldn't shake it. "And who do you think *you* are?"

I gulped. This guy was a little creepy. "Um, I'm Shauna Decker, sir."

"Riiiight…"

"Maybe I'd better be going."

"You're not a Christian, are you?"

OK. That just wasn't nice. He said it like it was a statement, not a question. I put my hands on my hips and looked up into his crinkly face. I have bright, red hair and freckles— and a bit of the spunk they say comes with both.

"As a matter of fact, I am," I said matter-of-factly.

"You don't look like it."

"Well, how's a Christian supposed to look?"

"You, young lady, are full of pride! I can tell!" he exclaimed, pointing a weathered finger in my face. He put his fingertips on my forehead and pushed my head down. "If you're a Christian, you should be humble! Remember: You're nobody special. You're just a sinner saved by God's grace. You're acting like a puffed-up flower instead of the little weed you are. You should be wearing one of these!" The old man spread out his arms, revealing his outfit. Was he wearing a potato sack?

I gulped. His words were strong, coming from years and years of experience. I examined my heart, looking for even a speck of pride. It didn't belong in my life, that I knew. Was I haughty? Could he be right? Who was I to contradict him?

Then…suddenly…I remembered who I was…

"Sir, with all due respect, *I am not a weed.* I've clothed myself with humility. And humility isn't a potato sack—it's a lifestyle of putting God first. To be *truly* humble is submitting to God and believing what *He* says over anything else I hear. He says I'm special. He says I'm unique. He says I should expect the best from Him because He will supply all my needs—and more!"*

I looked at him, standing there in that shabby, old sack. "Mr. Tradition, who's full of pride here? I'm just seeing myself as God sees me. But you…you're saying you need to live like a weed in a potato sack. You're living the opposite of what God says about you. Oh my!" I stepped back. "How full of pride is that?"

The old man just spat and stuttered and shifted his feet. I think the cat got his tongue. He nervously looked around. Then, with nothing more to say, he escaped in a flash, just as fast as he'd come.

I let out a long breath and said a prayer of thanks. I survived. The Holy Spirit gave me the Word that made old Mr. Tradition flee.

So I proceeded home, with my head held high—but not haughty. For, somehow, in the midst of it all, I discovered the truth that will forever keep me humble: Yes, I'm a flower, unique and special…but only because I was saved by grace when I was just another weed in a potato sack.

*Jeremiah 1:4; 1 Peter 5:5-6; Philippians 4:19

My Self-Image

22

**When Shane was confronted with two futures,
he knew which one to believe.**

One day I'm going to be a rancher. I may only be
11 years old, but I can see it. My sister, Shauna, says I'm too
imaginative, but what's wrong with that? I'm gonna have
horses and cattle and my very own ranch up on a hill.

That's what I was thinking about one day, during lunch,
when a kid sat down beside me and said, "No you won't."

"No, I won't what?" I asked.

"No, you won't have horses and cattle and your very
own ranch up on a hill," he said. "You won't be a rancher."

"How did you know I was thinking about that?" I wondered.

The boy simply replied, "I know everything you think.
I'm your self-image."

I looked around to see if anyone noticed this new kid. No one seemed to bat an eye. My self-image? I don't know... though he *did* look a lot like me, with freckles.

I decided to give him the benefit of the doubt. "So...what are you doing here?"

"Keeping you in check," he promptly replied with a wink. "Don't want you to get too big for your britches."

"How's that?"

"Just as I said. You're not going to own any horses or cattle. You're not going to be a rancher."

I was about to ignore this negative character when he pushed with the old "one-two."

"Think about it," he slammed. "You can barely ride a horse. And think of all the stupid things you've done. What makes you think you have what it takes to run a gigantic ranch?" Then he huffed and sighed and turned his back to me.

He did have a point. I had done a bunch of dumb things. What was I thinking? That I could actually be something great like a rancher? I'm not cut out for it.

Suddenly I heard a voice rise up from inside me. But I am.

I had heard that voice before. Often. And it was always worth listening to.

It said, *I am able to do more than you can imagine in your life. I am able to make your dreams come true. Have hope. Have faith. Have a ball. Remember—I am with you.**

Suddenly I could see it. I could see me riding a horse. Corralling the cattle. Sitting on the porch of my very own ranch—up on the hill. I tapped my self-image on the shoulder.

He skeptically turned my way. "I *have* made a lot of mistakes," I said, "but *my God* is with me. And with Him, I can do *all* things. He's put this dream in my heart—and it *will* happen!"*

"You can't do it," he said.

"I won't do it," I replied. "God will."

He looked furious. I winked at him and said, "Just keeping you in check." And with that, he completely disappeared.

Ever since then, whenever I think about the rich dream God's put in my heart, once in a while that kid will show up again. But I just remind him what God has said. And I'll keep reminding him until my poor self-image believes he's not poor anymore. He will have to believe it. It's the truth. For I'm going to be a rancher. I may only be 11 years old, but I can see it.

*Matthew 28:20; Philippians 4:13

My Best Friend, God

23

**When Shane was out of friends,
he found his Best Friend.**

When I came to Wichita Slim's town, things weren't easy. I was an orphan and Slim found a place for me to live and people who loved me...but I felt totally alone. There was no one *my age* around! Sure there was my sister Shauna, but she was three years younger than me and she could hardly talk.

Anyway you look at it I was alone, hoping for a friend. I'm sure I looked pitiful moping around town, talking to anyone who'd listen.

Then, after a whole summer alone, on my first day of school I met a kid named Nick.

Nick was pretty neat and he would eat lunch with me

when no one else would. We had a lot in common. We both liked horses and frogs, adventuring and telling jokes. And while it looked like I had *finally* found a best friend, something just wasn't quite right.

Sometimes when adults weren't around, Nick would curse—and I didn't like that. I also didn't like it when he said stuff about other kids...stuff I'm pretty sure wasn't true.

But, I figured, when friends are few and far between, you have to take what you can get. Besides, I hoped he'd start taking after me and stop doing some of those things.

Well it didn't happen. The last straw was when we were in class, taking a test and he whispered to me.

"Pssst! Shane! What's the answer to number three?"

"Huh?"

"Number three! What's the answer?"

I knew right then I had to make a decision. I could either whisper the answer back and keep a friend, or keep my mouth zipped shut...and possibly lose one.

I opened my mouth, but nothing came out. It couldn't. I realized that if I said *anything,* I would be disappointing another friend of mine...Jesus.

I knew Jesus didn't want me to cheat or help anyone else to cheat. I couldn't let *Him* down. So I said nothing. That was the last time Nick talked to me.

Suddenly I was without a friend again. No one to eat lunch with. No one to enjoy horses or frogs, and to share adventures or jokes with either.

I was alone. Totally alone.

You are not alone.

Those words came to me like whispered thunder.

You are not alone.

"God? Is that You?" I asked, sitting on the steps of my schoolhouse.

I am always with you. I will never leave you or abandon you, He reminded me, speaking to my spirit.*

At that moment I realized I had been looking in the wrong place for a best friend. Yes, it's important to have friends that build you up, but it's even more important to realize there is a Friend Who sticks even closer than a brother.*

It's God. He's my best friend. He enjoys horses and frogs, adventuring and telling jokes. He never asks me to cheat or talk about other kids behind their backs. He's a true friend.

That day on those steps, I decided to put Jesus first in my life. I made Him my top priority. And that's when things really turned around for me. As I spent time in prayer and reading God's Word each day, I became more like Him. And I began to make real friends—good friends— like Luis and Clara and even Billy Bob.

So that's my story. That's how I found my Best Friend. So if you're looking for a friend, a best friend, I have Someone I'd like to introduce you to.

It's *my* best friend...God.

*Hebrews 13:5; Matthew 6:33, 28:20; Proverbs 18:24

Prayer for Salvation

Father God, I believe that Jesus is Your Son and that You raised Him from the dead for me. Jesus, I give my life to You. Right now, I make You the Lord of my life and choose to follow You forever. I love You and I know You love me. Thank You, Jesus, for giving me a new life. Thank You for coming into my heart and being my Savior. I am a child of God! Amen.

About the Author

Christopher P.N. Maselli is the author of the *Commander Kellie and the Superkids*_{SM} series. He also writes the bimonthly children's magazine *Shout! The Voice of Victory for Kids*, and has contributed to the *Commander Kellie and the Superkids* movies.

Originally from Iowa and a graduate of Oral Roberts University, Chris now lives in Fort Worth, Texas, with his wife, Gena and their feline twins, Zoë and Zuzu, where he is actively involved in the children's ministry at his local church. When he's not writing, he enjoys collecting *It's a Wonderful Life* memorabilia, practicing Tae Kwon Do and constructing with Legos®.

Other Books Available

Baby Praise Board Book
Baby Praise Christmas Board Book
Noah's Ark Coloring Book
The *Shout!* Giant Flip Coloring Book
The *Shout!* Super-Activity Book
The *Shout!*Joke Book
The Best of *Shout!* Adventure Comics Book

*Commander Kellie and the Superkids*SM *books:*
Solve-It-Yourself Mysteries
The SWORD Adventure Book

*Commander Kellie and the Superkids*SM series
Middle Grade Novels by Christopher P.N. Maselli
#1 The Mysterious Presence
#2 The Quest for the Second Half
#3 Escape From Jungle Island
#4 In Pursuit of the Enemy
#5 Caged Rivalry
#6 Mystery of the Missing Junk

World Offices
of Kenneth Copeland Ministries

For more information about KCM and a free catalog,
please write the office nearest you:

Kenneth Copeland Ministries
Fort Worth, TX 76192-0001

Kenneth Copeland
Locked Bag 2600
Mansfield Delivery Centre
QUEENSLAND 4122
AUSTRALIA

Kenneth Copeland
Post Office Box 15
BATH
BA1 3XN
ENGLAND U.K.

Kenneth Copeland
Private Bag X 909
FONTAINEBLEAU
2032
REPUBLIC OF SOUTH AFRICA

Kenneth Copeland
Post Office Box 378
Surrey
BRITISH COLUMBIA
V3T 5B6   CANADA

UKRAINE
L'VIV 290000
Post Office Box 84
Kenneth Copeland Ministries
L'VIV 290000
UKRAINE

KENNETH COPELAND MINISTRIES

We're Here for You!

Shout!

Shout! The Voice of Victory for Kids is a Bible-charged, action-packed, bimonthly magazine available FREE to kids everywhere! Featuring *Wichita Slim* and *Commander Kellie and the Superkids*_{SM}, *Shout!* is filled with colorful adventure comics, challenging games and puzzles, exciting short stories, solve-it-yourself mysteries and much more!!

Stand up, sign up and get ready to *Shout!*

Believer's Voice of Victory **Television Broadcast***

Join Kenneth and Gloria Copeland, on the *Believer's Voice of Victory* broadcasts, Monday through Friday and on Sunday each week, and learn how faith in God's Word can take your life from ordinary to extraordinary. This is some of the best teaching you'll ever hear, designed to get you where you want to be—*on top!*

You can catch the *BVOV* broadcast on your local, cable or satellite channels.

*Check your local listings for times and stations in your area.

Believer's Voice of Victory **Magazine**

Enjoy inspired teaching and encouragement from Kenneth and Gloria Copeland each month in the *Believer's Voice of Victory* magazine. Also included are real-life testimonies of God's miraculous power and divine intervention into the lives of people just like you!

It's more than just a magazine—it's a ministry.

If you or some of your friends would like to receive a FREE subscription to Shout!, just send each kid's name, date of birth and complete address to:

Kenneth Copeland Ministries
Fort Worth, TX 76192-0001
Call:
1-800-600-7395
(9 a.m.-5 p.m. CT)
Or log on to our Web site at:
www.kcm.org